Cerebral Necrosis

Preframe

By Jaylen Woon

PREAMBLE

Before we get into things here, I must give special thanks to a few people. I couldn't have done it without my high-school teachers, shout out to Ryan Burgess and Carrie Frandoni, it was through their guidance that I was inspired to write this book series, and my parents who accompanied me through this endeavor. The story behind it all is that in my junior year of high school a contest was being held in my English class and my English teacher Mrs.Frandoni gave us the prompt for this writing contest. The prompt was the end of the world, make a story in 100 words exactly that describes a dystopian/post-apocalyptic future and/or present where the world is either ending or ended. My story ended up getting 2nd place in the national selection for the winners of this writing competition. Shortly after my teacher ended up recommending that if I wanted to I could expand on the story, make it a full book and fully flesh out my ideas on what I wanted it all to be. In truth this book was written with a bunch of common sci-fi pop-culture, like Cixin Liu's *wandering earth*, Dr.Who and the like but of course with my own twists on it.

Thus far this is my second book that I've ever written and I wanted to try a more experimental style of writing, which was inspired by another book that I read in my senior year English class called *"Illuminae"* by Amine Kaufman and Jay Kristoff, but also inspired based on the more conversational mannerisms present in the webcomic *"Homestuck"* Originally by Andrew Hussie but is really made by a bunch of people. I'm still new to writing a book and I'm still trying to improve my writing styles because a lot of the time my mind is all over the place.

Anyways, without further ado, go a head and enjoy the book

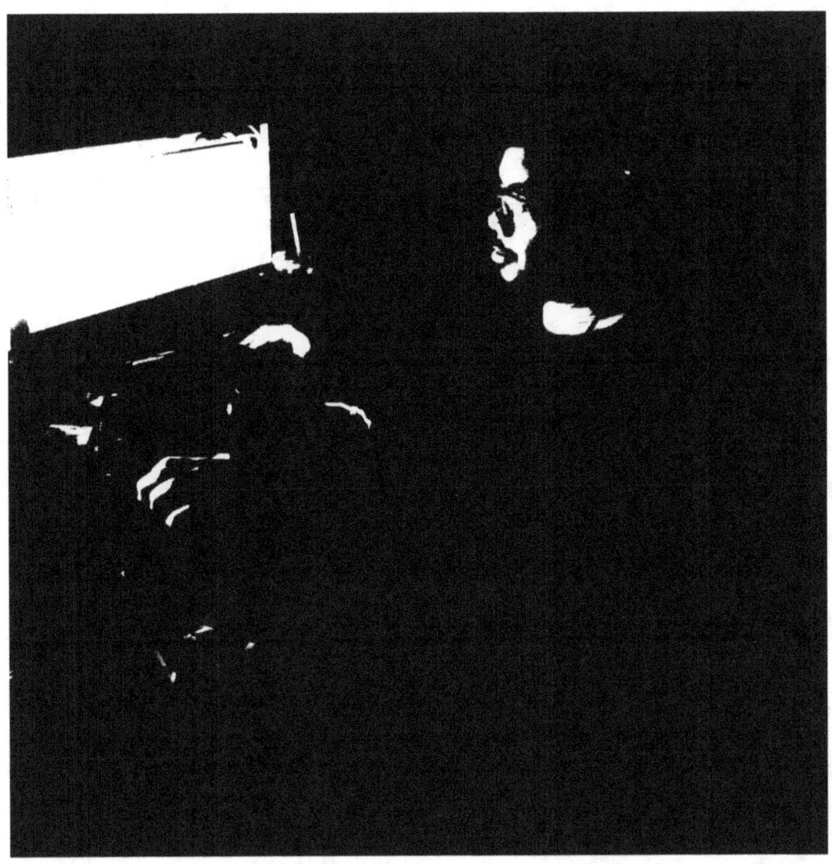

CHAPTER 0 REFRAME

As you start to read this book, you expect some kind of preamble, an explanation for what the beginning of this book is meant to be, but instead there's a black void with a very dim light in the distance. As that light fades in, giving the illusion of motion through a space where there is no reference, so does a figure of a man, at a computer. Then the man responds.

"Oh hello there, didn't think you'd ever be back here," he responds, "how about we do away with the narrator for a while?" Wait...what!? "Well, this is a preamble, the same one you were talking about, but in a different way. Instead of letting you do the explaining, how about I do the talking?" How could this man possibly do the explaining? Who does he think he is, the author? "...are we really going to do this right now...whatever just let me speak." Fine, if you want it to be that way.

"Ahem...actually, let me just do one last thing". **There we go, I no longer need to be constrained to those little things. Anyways, I bet you're wondering what's going on here. Let me explain. Ever since I shared with you my last story, I felt that the whole delivery was robotic, more standard and, pardon the pun, by the book. So let me just preface this and say that, this is going to be in a radically different style of writing. Don't worry, it's going to still make sense, but new inspirations and ideas have come to me this time, and I very much like this new kind of self-aware kind of style.**

Oh, right I almost forgot to introduce the book. This is a prequel story for the first book in the series. If you haven't read the last book, I recommend you do as it does outline this book perfectly.

The year is 2809, a whopping 210 years before the last story. Humanity is booming, countries are advancing, but foreign relationships are still shaky at best. Well, not amongst the big superpowers, but more along the lines of insurgents that always find a way to fight for something no matter how benevolent or small it may be

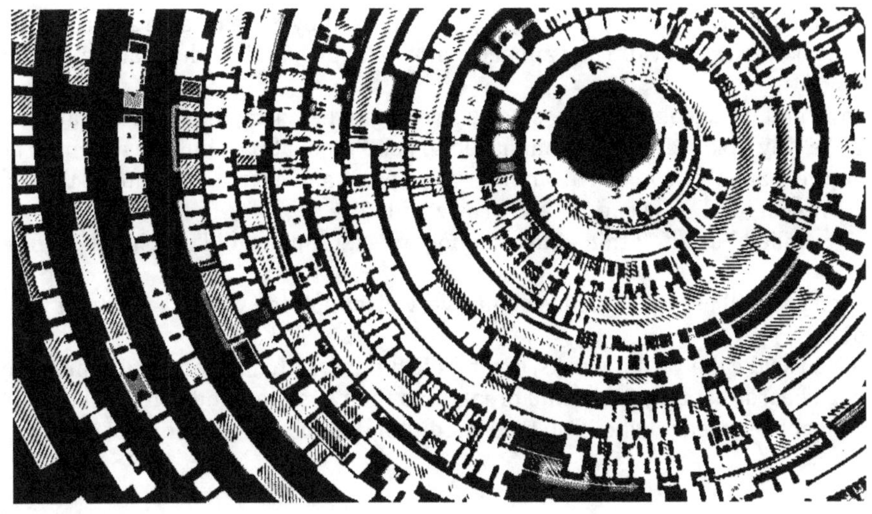

CHAPTER I THE CALL

Oh look, the first chapter. Well, without a further or do, take it away narrator.

Finally I get to do my job again - ahem, our story begins in the year 2809, 210 years before the events of the future unfold. **We already went over this.** Let me get to the point, please. **Ok, alright, I understand.** The year is 2809, 210 years before the tale of Eden and Lei, it's currently 00:00 in the White House on a Saturday night. The entire place is dark as it usually is because everyone's asleep, until the sound of a holo-phone with an urgent message tag on it. Basically, it sounds like an air raid siren that is loud enough to wake up a comatose person.

"uh...I'm up I'm up!", a man in the presidential suite shouts, "God damnit! It's too loud aaaa", the man then pulls out a drawer on his bedside table and slaps a button as he gets up out of bed and gets dressed for a meeting, and the hologram of a girl dressed in what appears to be a tuxedo appears,"huh?.....Wen?"

"Morning Mr.President, I understand that it's really early in America at this moment in time, but this is super urgent", she somehow calmly says with what appears to be an iron stare at the president,

"Ugh, can't this wait, I haven't even gotten my coffee ready", another holographic figure appears, this figure is sterner in stature, and is wearing a red blazer and has an eyepatch that has the flag of Russia on it,

" Come on Xertaif, comrade, it's so important that this is a call that is literally broadcast to the entire planet, it's actually on international TV", shouted the other figure

"Uhahhhhh, fine, what the hell is it", Xertaif said in a very disgruntled voice then Wen chimes in

"We are here to relay a message from the other world leaders, we are currently at war. I already know what you're going to say, at war with who, but this is why we're relaying a message. The other world leaders are currently in their respective capitol buildings urgently talking with their defense departments as all communications were sabotaged, only me and Vaschcroviz have managed to get comms back online. We also managed to get your comms back online because your systems are so esoteric and so easy to hack from across the world", she said in rapid succession, but with the clarity of a war general and the stern-ness of a leader

"We are at war with an organization that calls themselves nature's guardians, from reports from the other world leaders and even from captured spies within our borders, they appear to be an eco-terrorist group with origins coming from all over the world. They appear to not be happy at all with what we've done to the Earth, or so they say",

"What I don't understand is why they say we're ruining the Earth, that was the fault of the people from the 1800s all the way up to 2100, we've managed to keep them at bay, but they seem to be quite crafty with their stuff, they've managed to hijack our military weapons, and even armed nukes that have been put out of commission for well over 100 years", Vaschcroviz added.

"……oh shit", replied Xertaif, "I think I heard about this……..um…..hold on", he then goes to pull out his smartphone

"Oh dear god you still use that", said Wen in a very disappointed voice, "why don't you have a personal holo-orb?",

"Look", Xertaif said calmly, "if it works, don't fix it, anyways, thanks for the warning guys, I need to make a call to NASA, I heard that they had some break-in to their systems, and some unknown IDs have been entered in. There might be someone who is on the expedition that might not be one of ours",

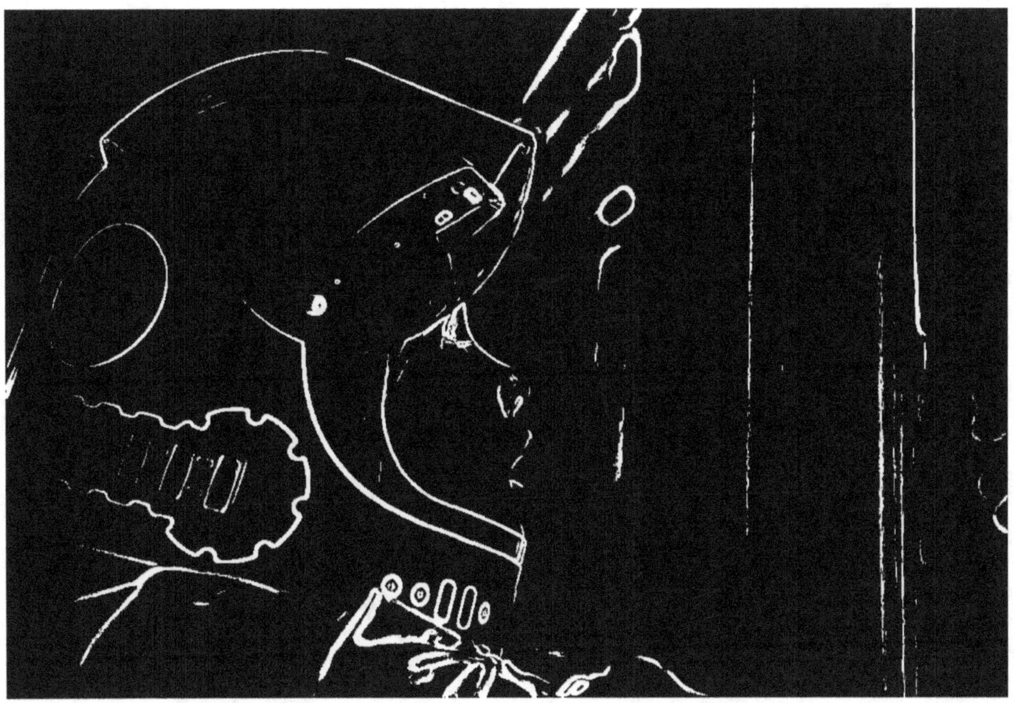

CHAPTER II AMONG US

Hey, buddy, let me take over for a bit. Why? what's the matter? **Your way of presenting things is boring, people don't want a bunch of flavor text that goes in-between hard to read sentences from characters heck we have no clue who's talking and when, and all you do is put he said or she said, or the name of the character said.** What do you propose then? **Have you ever heard of Homestuck**….what's that? **Exactly, so, WHOOOOSH**

Xertaif: **calling up the head of NASA** come on Vertis, pick up, I know it's midnight, but come on

Vertis: uhh, what is it Xertaif

Xertaif: it's an emergency. Someone may have boarded Zeus

Vertis: pshh, yeah right, we know there was a system breach and stuff was changed around, but I seriously doubt there's something going on. Why so paranoid all of a sudden?

Xertaif: Wen and Vas A. not only blared the super ultra-mega "oh my god we're all going to die" alarm, but they also broadcasted that whole ordeal worldwide. We are at war with some weird bio-terrorist group, and there seems to be spies there

Vertis: I highly doubt that they would go on an expedition to space, because if they really love the earth so much, they wouldn't leave it

Xertaif: I don't know man; we need to contact the ship and ask them to check for anyone that's suspicious

Vertis: um…. ok…..I'll do that…after I get coffee

Xertaif: yeah..I need coffee
too………
………**HEY!**
Let me do it **NO!** Come on **WHY!** Because, you just put names and text. There's no finesse, no detail added to it, and you split the conversation up too much. You need nice, neat concise blocks of text, then you denote what character it belongs to, and thus you can provide a bunch of detail to the story and……..…. **ok, good got rid of him, hopefully that's the last we see of him, his style of storytelling is too robotic, too standard, plus I personally find this easier to read. Anyways, back to the chapter. Oh, and I should set the scene to this part; we're on U.U.W Zeus doing social deduction**

Arroh: **doing his check in task**. This is Arroh Y. Youkote of the U.U.W. Zeus, the time is approximately 13:00. Come in command, over

Cevko: Commander Cevko responding. we read you loud and clear, Lieutenant Youkote. What is the current status report on sector 5?

Arroh: sector 5 systems nominal.

Cevko: report what systems

Arroh: life support wiring is no longer frayed, and the door power fuse is no longer blown, power has been rerouted to accel 3

Cevko: confirmed, continue to monitor Lieutenant

Arroh: commander, may I ask what this is all for?

Cevko: that information is classified, all crew will be briefed when the time is right

Arroh: alright, well, Arroh Y. Youkote signing off

Cevko: over and out

Zara: Mayday! Mayday! This is Captain Zara of sector 8,

Cevko: wait, captain? But only Lieutenants run sectors. Unless….

Zara: that is what I'm here to report sir, Lieutenant Iwoke is dead. He was discovered by Private Marrik at 12:59 and reported to me within the minute.

Cevko: alright…ahem…. All crew aboard the Zeus, please report to crew annex 0, this is not a drill. I repeat this is not a drill

in crew annex 0, all the crew members all 9 of them gather around a table and the commander is pacing back and forth around a white board

Cevko: Roll call. Lieutenant Youkote

Arroh: reporting

Cevko: Captain Uiomwe

Zara: reporting

Cevko: private Marrik

Eiensta: Reporting

Cevko: Lieutenant Copperfeld

Roger: Roger

Cevko: Lieutenant Burgess

Ryan: reporting

Cevko: Lieutenant Frandoni

Carrie: reporting

Cevko: Lieutenant Swain

Chase: reporting

Cevko: Lieutenant Furguson

Michael: reporting

Cevko: alright, here's the situation, Captain Uiomwe reported that Private Marrik found Lieutenant Iwoke dead at 12:59

Roger: could've just been a mishap, Arroh, you said life support systems were flakey

Arroh: yep, main power cable was frayed

Ryan: what could've caused it to fray?

Arroh: that's what I'm questioning, because when I found it the cables seemed almost freshly frayed by hand

Cevko: exactly, I just received a message from space command that there may be an impostor or two onboard

they all start looking worried

Cevko: this is why I'm activating the "walk the plank" doctrine, anyone deemed as suspicious and/or caught in the act of trying to sabotage this mission will be flushed out of the airlock, all decisions will be made on a simple majority vote. Any objections

Chase: Sir, if I may?

Cevko: go ahead

Chase: what if we make a wrong choice and the person ejected isn't an impostor

Cevko: then we have to live with it, we have no way of telling who is or isn't the impostors, the only way we could possibly tell is to check it over with space command, but that would take days for information to reach us

Michael: this is stupid, why do we have to look for an impostor

Chase: sus

Michael: no, hear me out, hear me out. We just wait to see if someone does something bad

Arroh: I suggest we try to watch after the commander

Cevko: why is that?

Arroh: the commander always has the highest security clearance, and will be able to override our current permissions, if an impostor is going to take out someone it'd be the commander

Cevko: good point. Anyway, you all have tasks to do in order to keep this ship afloat, so-to-speak. Meeting dismissed

fast forward a couple of minutes and change the setting to the reactor core, Ryan ends up seeing a weird shadow near the reactor control panel and then the reactor starts to go into meltdown mode

Ryan heads to the reactor control panel and starts trying to reset the reactor

[REDACTED]: **starts sneaking up behind Ryan but the door to the reactor room started to open, so he quickly jumps into the nearest ventilation shaft**

Chase: hey, you ok? I heard the meltdown alarm

Ryan: I saw something or someone here messing with the reactor, I just fixed it

Chase: are you sure? You're the only one in here

Ryan: I think whatever it was hopped into the vent over there

Chase: **heads over to the vent and shakes it a bit**. Damnit, whatever it is can open vents quickly and quickly close vents and seals them. This vent is a bit loose compared to last time I had to crawl in it

Ryan: the only way for something to be able to do that is for it to have a tool that can quickly drill the screws, let alone fit them

Chase: alright, I think we have a lead - someone with a octahedral shaped drill bit and a drill would be suspect here

Ryan: do you know anyone with such a thing?

Chase: no, but we could check storage logs to see when last a tool like that was checked out

meanwhile in sector 8 where electrical and accel 1 and accel 2 is

Zara: what the hell **looks at the engine's control panel** why is that off, this console is locked to us

Eiensta: hey Captain, look at this

Zara: huh?

there's a mass of cables and random metal strewn across the floor near that sector's joint lock

Eiensta: whoever the impostor is, they seem to know how to take apart the ship

Zara: that's impossible; no one knows how this ship was actually built besides the commander, but he's not qualified to dis-assemble it

Eiensta: whatever the case may be, let's try and fix it before this sector depressurizes

the emergency alarm starts to blare across the entire ship

Cevko: ok who called the meeting

Carrie: that'd be me, Michael is dead. We were both in sector 1 refilling the EVA gear's oxygen tank, I went to go and get a wrench to properly seal some of the loosened oxygen sealers, but when I came back he was dead

Ryan: do you by chance have an Octahedral drill?

Carrie: no

Chase: storage logs state that you were the last one to enter storage, and that you checked out an Octahedral drill

Carrie: I was in storage, but again that was for the wrench….wait why are you asking if I know about that kind of drill?

Ryan: we found someone in reactor who started a meltdown, but before I could get a good look at them they jumped into a vent

Chase: Ok, where was everyone else?

Zara: I was with Eiensta in sector 8 trying to figure out why the engines got mis-aligned

Eiensta: I can vouch for that, and it seems like someone also tried to sabotage the joint to that sector

Roger: I think I saw Arroh head to sector 8 before you

Arroh: that is true, but that was because I was busy at each power junction trying to accept new re-directed powers to life support

Zara: he wasn't the one that did any of that, power junction NT-2000 wasn't anywhere near accel panel 2 and the sector joint

Eiensta: what about Cevko? where was he during all this?

Chase: the commander? Why the hell are you throwing sus at him

Eiensta: because he's not exactly a saint either, he's still another person on this ship, and I need to ask, where was the commander?

Cevko: I was at security trying to look for any previous logs of breaches and/or sabotages and where any commands like that were being sent from

Eiensta: that's lies, remember, I'm the security officer, I set up cameras in security to make sure security is secure

Cevko: are you sure? I checked and those cameras aren't turned on

Eiensta: yes they are

Cevko: no they weren't

Eiensta: plus, as Ryan and chase reported someone hopped into the vent in the reactor, and tried to look at storage logs. I remember there was a bug with the storage logs where you can erroneously read an ID number and it be linked with someone else's name, what's even more damning is that you were the one that reported this bug to me, and the fact that the impostor also happened to have that shape of drill to get through the vents that fast implies that something had to be taken out of storage first. Chase, when you checked logs did you notice anything funny

Chase: now that you mention it, I saw 2 entries from Carrie that were timed weirdly. The first one was her checking out the Octahedron drill, and the other one was checking out the monkey wrench, but the ID numbers were slightly different

Eiensta: that's why I say that it's the commander because there's the most evidence to support that claim

Cevko: but you're missing a few points there in your argument

Eiensta: ok what is that?

Cevko: I'm the commander with the highest security clearance and I have the power to make it so that none of you can access anywhere on this ship

Eiensta: true, but how do we know you're just not trying to string us along so that you can do so later

Cevko: We've been on this ship for 3 god damn years. If I were stringing any of you along I would've logically executed this plan that I supposedly have in year 2

Carrie: it's Eiensta

Eiensta: WHAT!?

Carrie: think about it, you were the first to find Lieutenant Iwoke dead, and based on the time you reported it, it almost seemed like you knew he was dead before he was dead

Zara: but he reported it to me

Carrie: exactly, he probably reported it to you so that it looks like he's following the chain of command in order to not appear sus, but think about the timelines. if you reported Iwoke's dead body at 13:00 and Eiensta actually found it and told you about it at 12:59, then don't you think that it's a bit sus that he reported it so quickly.

Zara:.....um............

Carrie: everyone, submit your votes

after a voting ballot has been cast the computer then shows the results

Eiensta: damnit!

Cevko: the votes have spoken, Eiensta is first to be subjected to the "walk the plank" doctrine

Eiensta: **gets pushed to the air lock**

Chase: any last words Eiensta?

Eiensta: you've doomed the earth, you've doomed nature, and worst of all, you doomed yourselves, Viacondios **opens the air lock and almost voluntarily jumps out of it**

Zara: **closes the air lock** damn, I had no clue that Eiensta was the impostor

Cevko: I'll go and send a transmission to space command about this right now, for now we need to give Iwoke and Michael a proper burial

meanwhile back on earth and in the NASA war room facility

Xertaif: right, I called you all here today because we are in some deep trouble right about now. I know it has been years since we had to use this room, but this is what we need now. Recent communications with Russian Premiere Vaschcroviz Ventriov and Chinese president Wen Jay-Zhou suggests that there may be insurgents with an agenda to "reclaim nature" have infiltrated many states, and that there may be impostors among us. This is why I've invited only the people I trust, and the people that I've known since before the whole eco-terrorist movement started.

Vertis:……well you obviously know me because I'm your cousin, but who the hell are the rest of these people

Xertaif: well, let's start from the right and go to the left. First is Lieutenant Zen Wan-Lu, he was one of my classmates back in college, and he joined the military a few years before I was elected

Wan-Lu: nice to see you again old friend

Xertaif: nice to see you too. Next is Ambassador Nawoe, he was my pen-pal from back in high-school when I did a student exchange program to Ethiopia

Nawoe: hello all of you people

Xertaif: and finally my vice president, Maiora Agee, she was one of the biggest inspirations of my life back in college, as she was always the best at debates, getting people on the same page, and figuring out how psychology, science, education, tribalism, and current circumstances fit into politics

Maiora: and I know what you may be wondering, why is this current meeting only full of friends of the president. It's quite simple, it has nothing to do with any kind of ulterior motive, psychologically and statistically speaking someone you've known for longer and known from before any ideologic movement started tend to be less likely to be in the movement and if they were are more likely to exhibit behavior that would be deemed out of the ordinary. Basically, he chose you all because it's easier to detect if you are an impostor or not

Wan-Lu: so what's the situation commander

Xertaif: the situation is this. As a said briefly earlier, there has been some infiltrations going on around the world. Remember that system breach we had a few years ago, months before we launched Project Zeus rising?

Vertis: yeah, what about it

Xertaif: well, Wen had her people hack into our systems and figured out what went wrong

Nawoe: wait she can do that?

Maiora: yes, and very easily. Basically because of the culture surrounding technological movement here in

America our computer systems and computer system security has lagged behind the international standard for years, and the programmers and/or hackers in Mainland China are just better at being aware of technological advantages and weaknesses. Basically, they can do that because our tech is old and outdated and they have the best programmers in the world.

Xertaif: oof, anyways. Based on the system information that Wen was able to get from us, she confirmed that the system breach we had wasn't a data leak, it was a data injection

Vertis: why didn't I know about that?

Xertaif: let's be real here, none of us knew that it was a data injection, plus you're just management over here, either the systems team didn't catch it, or they might have been infiltrated as well and either are all impostors or are being blackmailed into not telling us about it, that's why for now it's best to allow Wen and her people to continue to gather information from the outside.

Wan-Lu: so what do you want us to do?

Xertaif: Zen, you have ties in Taiwan correct?

Wan-Lu: yes

Xertaif: I want you to deliver a message to Zau Ha, let them be hacked by China, because their security teams may have also been compromised, same thing to you Nawoe, if we want to solve this crisis we have to do it covertly

Maiora: should I notify the CIA

Xertaif: no, I know very damn well that the CIA is no longer of use to us. They've kept their ways of wanting money in exchange for allegiance. Knowing the insurgents, they probably have a lot of money, and bribed the CIA with it. So no, don't notify that cesspool

Vertis: I should send a transmission to the crew of the Zeus from my personal terminal

Xertaif: no, **handing him his phone,** use this, under amendment 680 the president's personal devices can't be monitored by anyone, and plus it's not actually compatible with the Zed-1039 protocol, it can't be contacted by anything besides equipment that can use the 802.1200 data transmission protocol

Vertis: jesus christ, how old is this thing?

Xertaif: it was my grandfather's phone so....way older than any of us

Maiora: alright, you all have your missions, go safely

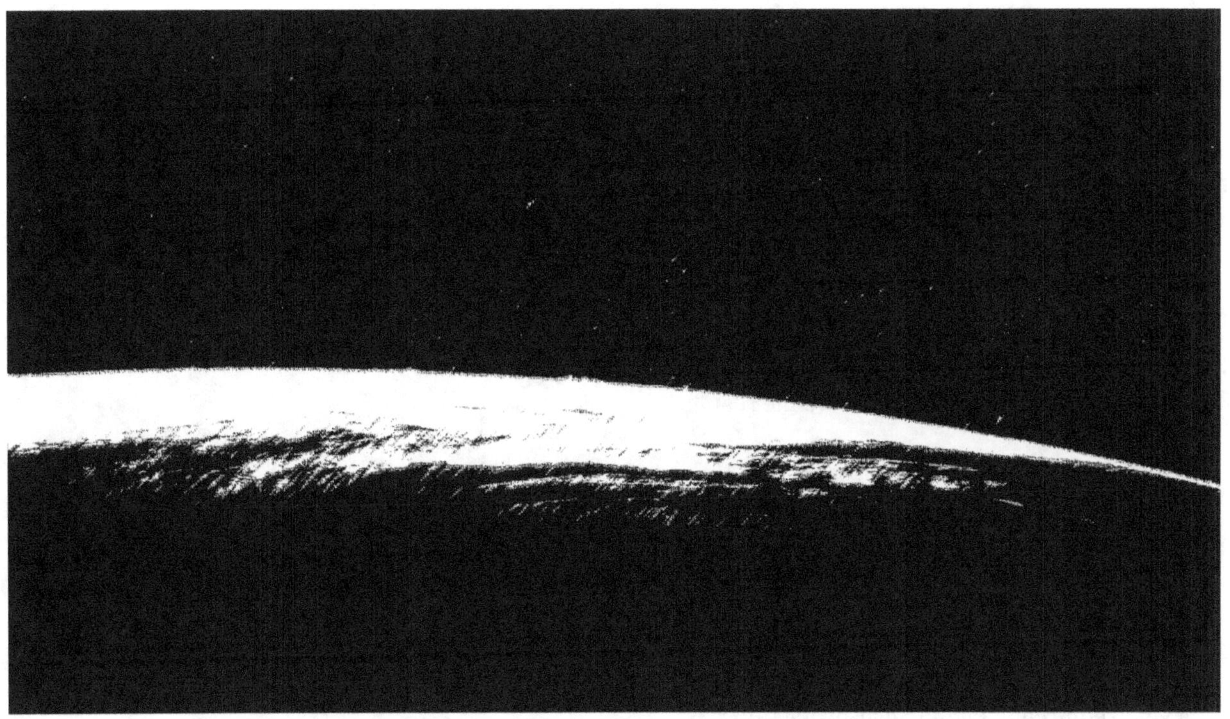

CHAPTER III ARRIVAL

As time went on, more and more insurgent campaigns and what could be considered coups started going on more and more, though since each nation has plans in place to prevent coups and when a coup is staged, they actually can figure out its source and purpose. They basically had to roll in the military to stop it as all the coups that started popping up around the globe were by this eco-terrorist group wanting to basically destroy mankind because they believe that mankind is ruining the earth, though in the year 2809 pollution is negative. In the year 2120 all countries started to move towards greener energy sources, and started replacing incineration with recycling, so by 2800 the earth, though already damaged by the generations of pollution and the like from the early 1800s all the way up to 2090, was improving, but the eco-terrorist group believe that humanity just shouldn't exist.

Anyways, enough with the back story. Let's fast-forward to 1 more year in the future and now we're with the crew of the U.U.W. Zeus, and they actually are in orbit of Trappist-1e-2 which is the most habitable planet found there even though almost all the planets orbiting the star are habitable

Cevko: All of you, to positions

Arroh: Orbit around Trappist-1e-2 secured

Carrie: Life support systems nominal

Chase: EVA equipment nominal

Zara: initiating lander launch procedure

Roger: docking lock dis-engaged

Ryan: heat shield properly aligned

Cevko: alright, brace for planet fall

they launch the lander which is sort of based off of the Tienwen-2 rover launched in 2020 where it has a rocket boosted platform with it's intended payload on top of it, and an orbiter meant to gather and process data. They reach the planet's surface after a bumpy atmospheric entry

Cevko: Zara, climate check

Zara: launching probes……..ok here are the results

Pressure: 1 atm
Composition: 20% CO2, 40% Nitrogen 40% Oxygen
Solar Radiation per hour: 432 quintillion
Greenhouse effect: unknown
Soil composition: 80% Nitrates, 20% unknown
Flora: Super-earthlike
Wildlife: Super-earthlike
surface composition: 70% Soil 30% water
EVA gear requirement: Mild Solar protection

Chase: so we just need sun screen

Zara: basically, anyways, launching automated settlement construction droids

another time-skip this time a few days into the future to when they have a habitat, and a research facility fully set up, and have already captured some wildlife and did some ethical research on them

Zara: Captain Zara Uiomwe, 31st of December 2809, Entry 1:

     This journal was created by me in order to provide documentation for when we head back to earth. We started our journey on the 1st of January 2805. Our mission was to travel to the closest system that we could get to in a reasonable amount of time which was Trappist-1e, now of course it's 1 light year away from home, at our current speeds and rate of acceleration it would be impossible to get here in almost 5 years, what the brilliant people of earth did was band together in a sense of solidarity and worked tirelessly for god knows how long making the United Unified World Zeus. The first ever interstellar manned object. It was assembled in space as almost 4 million+ Kilograms of fuel and titanium would be next to impossible to build on earth without causing massive damage to its crust. On the day of its completion the best and the brightest of each military branch and scientific arm of the government was chosen for its maiden voyage. Armed with the latest tech humanity had to offer, the most powerful and long lasting rocket engines ever, and state of the art fuel-less correction propulsion we then were instructed to use the RCS thrusters to fly and do a gravity assisted slingshot around the Sun, Earth, Mars, and Jupiter in order to start off with solar escape velocity and accelerate with the literal tons and tons of rockets strapped to us.

     Almost half-way through our journey we receive info from command that there may be an impostor aboard the ship, and he started killing off crew members in order to take control of the whole mission, that impostor was private Eiensta Marrik, after being found out he was swiftly ejected from the airlock and thus confessed that he was the imposter. Now that we have safely arrived at Trappist-1e-2 we've set up a habitat and a research facility, we've captured some of the local wildlife in order to study it. Will post another update when that whole thing is done.

Carrie: Lieutenant Carrie Frandoni, 20th of January 2810, Entry 2:

This planet is absolutely wonderful, and remarkably interesting. We have been examining the geological formations, flora, and wildlife that inhabit this planet. I think one of the most interesting discoveries with our time here is the wildlife because of the way they react to us. On the surface they all seem to be quadruped and mostly feline and/or K-9 in nature but they do not contain such DNA to be counted as such. Alongside that they have exhibited extraordinary signs of intelligence that gives human intelligence a good run for its money. Even compared to dolphins these creatures are smart beyond what we would have ever imagined. As such, instead of resorting to standard research procedures, we managed to teach these creatures how to talk, and how to do more with their stature. Now they have their own habitat that was built based on a blueprint of our own habitat; however, it wasn't our own machines that built it for them - instead we let them walk around our habitat, gave them materials, and proceeded to build their habitat with psionic abilities. Upon further and more detailed examination, their biology is the most bizarre that I've ever seen. They have more or less the same systems as actual cats and dogs back on earth, that much is to be expected, because the conditions where these lives started was more or less like earth, but it appears that due to the extra nutrients and exotic composition of their DNA they have a super developed brain, that could do what we always concluded was impossible.

Further analysis is required in order to make a full understanding of these weird alien creatures, but said further analysis will prove to be easy, because we can literally ask if they want to volunteer for these examinations and usually, they say yes, because they've seen how we adapted our facilities to their almost human-like needs. Heck, some want to actually come back to Earth with us just to see what it's like. I hope they don't get space sick easily, because it'd be very good to bring a few back to Earth for a more thorough examination with better equipment

Ryan: Lieutenant Ryan Burgess, 1st of April 2810, Entry 3:

These creatures, Triessians, as they like to be called, are literally the best thing ever.
Back on Earth, I use to teach new NASA employees and interns how technology systems work, from the old stuff from all the way back in the 1960s all the way up to the current year tech, and never once in my entire life did anyone grasp these concepts more easily than the Triessians. It's to the point where sometimes they help us repair any electronic that has been damaged or worn out and usually better than we can. They would be great to have aboard the ship, especially since there's only 7 of us left and the ship was designed to be able to support about 1000 people, so we have a bunch of room. Oh, and let's not forget about their innate abilities of telekinesis; really handy when it comes to a lot of small tasks, I wonder if they can teach us this?

Arroh:Lieutenant Arroh Youkote, 4th of May 2810, Entry 4:

IakoidoMuityiaZenkgzi, Konichiwa, Hello. Yes, the Triessians are quickly innovating on things. When we first came here, they were wild animals not because they did not have intelligence, but because they had no reference on what language was. When we taught them English, Japanese, and Chinese, they could speak it very well, but the way they spoke it almost seemed like they were just playing with the language until today when they invented their own new one. Ironically just like humans they don't like their own language because it can be very difficult to learn, this one tenfold because it consists of the grammar rules of English, with the sentence structure of Japanese, and the intonations and context-based words of Chinese. They also seem to have developed their own culture almost overnight. I guess Ryan had a huge effect over them because their culture now revolves around technology, not as a religion, but as a needed tool of life. Heck, they even started fabricating their own tools that work better for a quadruped than they ever could for a human. These creatures are remarkable.

Chase: Lieutenant Chase Swain, 10th of June 2810, Entry 5:

How are they so good at ultra-fighter 19…and every other video game I play with them

Roger: Lieutenant Roger Copperfeld, 13th of November 2810 Entry 6:

this entry seems garbled and incomplete, but there's only two words that can be seen
It was him

Cevko: Commander Cevko Iyankovitch formerly known as Cevko Inovo, 1st of December 2810, Entry 7:

Mission was successful, specimens are secured on board and we've left that planet, to be honest I'm surprised those god damn animals didn't try to stop me from killing those buffoons, though I guess one sort of did get away. Anyways, when I get back, I expect double pay, after all these stupid mutts are trying to tear this damn ship apart - good thing the good ol' fashion shock collar can keep them at bay. Viacondios

CHAPTER IV UNKNOWN BATTLEGROUNDS

obviously since we were last at earth it had been a year or so as shown by the documentation logs by the now deceased crew of the U.U.W Zeus. In that time, a lot of the world leaders have managed to claw back control over their own countries, but in order to do so, they had to formally declare a state of martial law. With this comes with a lot of division, fear, etc. Here we are with the president of the United States giving a speech about this

Xertaif: Ladies and gentlemen of the union. It is a rough time in American history; heck I think this is the roughest time there is. As many of you may know, I have enacted martial law under unanimous congressional approval. I know you may be watching this from home, work, or wherever, and are scared. Scared of not only the fact that your freedoms are limited, and that your streets are being patrolled by the military. I rest assure you that you are safe and sound when these policies are in place. As many of you may know, there is unlawful insurrection going on at this moment in time, not just here in this country but all over the world. These people who seek to dismantle the peace and unity between the nations that took so long to build claim that they're doing all these actions for the sake of nature, that regardless of how much we try to appease them, by switching to greener and renewable sources of energy, making recycling a mandatory requirement, making strict laws meant to protect not only humans but also animals from abuse, basically bending to their every will. Just because we walk along this beautiful planet, they deem us as a blight. So please my fellow Americans, I beg of you, don't let this get out of hand. Don't be afraid of the authority that has been deployed as they are only trying to help you, and to keep you safe, and on the flip side, don't turn this situation into the red scare from all those centuries ago. I want you all to treat each other as equals, as human beings who deserve unity. The power to punish people for their wrong doings isn't in your hands, it's in my hands, for it is my sworn duty to protect every American in this country. With that I bid you farewell, and remember. United we stand, divided we fall.

Maiora: Xertaif, we have a situation

Xertaif: what is it?

Maiora: I just got off the phone with the secretary of defense and the head of homeland security. 500 world war III style submarines just surfaced off the coast of Maryland, each cannot be identified, reports state that they seem to be world war III Japanese submarines that have been given a serious upgrade and a new paint job

Xertaif: ok, they're just submarines, just launch the rail ships and take care of them

Maiora: that's the thing sir, they are armed with nova bombs

Xertaif: what the hell, 1 can level 5 cities at once, but 500!? Where did they get this technology

Maiora: based on reported long-range scans, they appear to have gotten the submarines from Japan, but the Nova bombs were fabricated on their own

Xertaif: that's impossible, all plans for the Nova bombs were destroyed after world war III, and all the Nova Bombs globally were all disassembled and their materials used to build Zeus

Maiora: unfortunately we have no information on how they re-developed such an esoteric weapon. The real question is why the hell do the japanese still have war machines

Xertaif: it was a treaty deal after world war III, all countries were to vow to fully demilitarize unless it's a country that either can't be protected by another country's perimeter AA systems, or a country that doesn't have the economical capacity to support its own

Maiora: so it's like the military that we have?

Xertaif: it's like the military all countries have, none are active duty unless either being drafted for NASA or the other equivalents, being called in for martial law, or a war breaks out. Usually, it's only the first option that the military gets called for. We've never had to call a martial law or fight a war for well over 600 years. Whatever these terrorists are doing, they seem well trained

Maiora: should I instruct homeland security to divert grid power?

Xertaif: yes, but tell them to divert it to the point laser defense, shields, and long range jamming radars

Maiora: Aye sir...hold on **she holds her finger up to her ear like she's listening to someone** just got the latest reports from homeland security, we need to get to the war room, everyone is trying to call you

Xertaif: **sigh** prepare my holo-receptor, I'm going to get an extra strong cup of the finest Martian coffee

Maiora: sir, we're out of that

Xertaif: I have a secret stash of coffee grown throughout the entire solar system

Maiora: care to share?

Xertaif: why should I?

Maiora: because everyone here is basically addicted to coffee

Xertaif: sure, I'll go get the bags, it's up to you to make your own coffee, and the Martian blend is mine

After an epic coffee making montage with everyone putting in too much creamer into their coffee while the president literally makes home-made death wish coffee almost, we head to the war room, a room that though it looks clean and new, hasn't been used in over 100 years. It doesn't even have more up-to-date stuff; it just looks like the war room as it was in the year 2020 as it never got any updates leading up to World War III, and it was never touched again afterwards besides from some cleaning crews that kept the place from filling up with cobwebs

Holo-receptor: Channel 0xfffff – 0xFFFFF closed, Channel 0x45 opened and secured using R.E.S.A.L.T quantum encryption. Waiting for Quantum state $|\bar{a}(t*d)\rangle = \sum_n C_n(t*d)| \text{🌀🌀}_n\rangle == \sum_\infty \text{Matrix.Result}()$

Xertaif:...whelp, time to wait a billion years for anyone to join, because highest level security there is **sips coffee**

Wen: already hacked it
Xertaif: **spits out some of his coffee** how do you keep doing this!?

Wen: we have the fastest quantum computer in the world, and you're still using the first one America came up with back in 2100, so of course we'd be able to get in quickly

Xertaif: well, you kind of didn't hack it, that quantum state is so very specific that the only way for it to be hacked is to already know it

Wen: well, not really, but it's on such an obscure channel you kind of have to know where to look

Xertaif: where's Vas

Wen: He's dealing with security issues on his own, expect him to take a while because he's using fort Knox level encryption, which may take a while to get to the correct state

Xertaif: whatever, is there anyone else joining

Wen: well yes, and no **more figures start appearing in the chairs of the round conference room type building, but they don't seem to be blipping in, they seem to be walking in**

Xertaif:wha

Wen: these are what's left of each fallen country's government, Vice Chancellor of Germany Maeinstauf Goauten

Maein: most just call me Maein, pleased to meet your acquaintance Mr.USA

Wen: First man of france Fidel Lorrene

Fidel: Bonjour comment allez-vous monsieur Xertaif

Xertaif: Ça va tres bien, et vous?

Fidel: Ça va tres mal

Xertaif: I can guess why

Wen: Deputy prime minister of Canada Maraniece Kontare

Maran: how are you doing down there neighbor, obviously better than us because I was ran out of my own country

Xertaif:....any more coming soon?

Wen: nope, that's it, the other governments have either completely fallen and has to resort to living in a bunker, or entirely destroyed because the leaders were tied to a tree and given nothing but bitter almonds and having the word of the tree god or whatever shouted at them

Xertaif: figures that this is a religion. Those things should've died out in 2700, I guess one managed to survive

Wen: whatever the case may be, we have spies out trying to rescue the rest of the VIPs

Vas: oh, hello comrades. Wen, why other people here

Wen: these are what remains of the world

Vas: ah, I see. We have new report. Suicide of terrorists

Xertaif: wait what?

Wen: these eco-terrorists have some really strange tech, like for instance, they fired this bomb at Egypt, initial scans said that these were World War III era bombs, but when they hit it started rapidly turning the entirety of Africa into a jungle, and shortly afterwards the terrorists killed everyone that was alive in all of Egypt, then killed themselves

Maein: it's a suicidal religion? Das not goot, out of all the religions to survive the 2700 cultural shift a stupid vone like zat survived

Maran: that's why I asked Ms.Wen here to organize this meeting, we see that you have your defense systems up, and have a bunch of those seed subs at your coast

Fidel: **takes out his phone and texts xertaif**

Xertaif: ok, Fidel has some input on this, but he can't speak English so he's having me translate.
He's saying that he knows where these bombs are coming from

Vas:.....you do?

Xertaif: he says that the bombs were an experiment in 2790 to try and combat climate change, these bombs were scrapped because compared to the other climate altering tech we have these were highly invasive and destructive

Maein: May I ask, who was the vone zat made this contraption?

Xertaif: it was a joint effort between everyone in the world, supposedly the lab that was doing the whole research was long forgotten in the south pole.

Wen: wow, a full 20 years before I became chairmen, I wonder what was going through Yi Zhoumeng's head at the time

Xertaif: apparently he was the one that decided to can the project, because he explained what might happen if there's any WMDs in the world, especially after WWIII

Maran: so let me get this straight, Presidents, Chancellors, etc from 2790 was like "oh right bud let's just use bombs to change the climate eh" and never once thought about the consequences of literally a bomb

Wen: and it took someone educating the rest of those leaders about world war III to sway them into stopping the project

Holo-receptor: Warning, un-known state trace-back signature detected, attempting to reroute

Xertaif: wait what

Maiora: **bursts into the room spilling her cup of coffee** SIR, WE'RE BEING HACKED BY THAT SUBMARINE SQUADRON

Xertaif: GET THE ZEROS ON IT, NOW!

Wen: **she's very sternly and shouting at someone in Chinese** DAMNIT, HOW DID THEY GET PAST OUR SECURITY AS WELL

Xertaif: IT'S THE HOLO LINK, ZENO, ACTIVATE SHUT DOWN PROCEEDURE

Zeno: shut down procedure cannot be initiated while re-routing the quantum link

Xertaif: SELF-DESTRUCT THEN

Zeno: command locked

Xertaif: SOMEONE, SHUT DOWN THAT GOD DAMN HOLO-PROJECTOR

> **another holographic figure appears, and all of the other holograms get grouped in the chairs that are closer to Xertaif because there's like 50 chairs all in a circle and the entire conference table is a giant circle with an empty space in the middle, so they get grouped around him, and the new holographic figure fades in more.**
> **The figure has what appears to be a robe similar to that seen in countless cliché sci-fi films, but woven out of silken leaves with an insignia of planet earth embroidered on the left side of the chest.**

?: Auf wiedersehen, Ni hao, Bonjour, hello.

Vas: no Russian?

?: I don't know Russian, anyways, I'm here to ask you for something

Xertaif: hey, before you start making demands, I want to know your name

?: you're not going to be getting my name

Xertaif: BULLSHIT, YOU HACK INTO MY COMMUNICATION SYSTEM AND WALK IN LIKE YOU OWN THE PLACE, I HAVE THE RIGHT TO KNOW YOUR GOD DAMN NAME, AND DON'T DO THAT MOVIE CLICHÉ OF GIVING ME A DAMN CODE NAME, WHO ARE YOU AND WHY ARE YOU TRYING TO MURDER ALL OF HUMANITY

Kiola: Fine, if you must, my name is Kiola wadffafjaoifjofieieojf

Xertaif: wait what?

Kiola: I don't know how to translate my last name into your languages, frankly human language is stupid

Xertaif: ok, so you're one of the alien races that we've attracted, why are you trying to kill us all

Kiola: because, you humans are a blight on this planet, of all planets

Xertaif: and who gives you the authority to dictate that?

Kiola: My race is the warawrjariarajrair, or translated to English, it should roughly translate to the Natura Hominies Arum

Maein: that's latin

Kiola: same difference, anyways if you must know, My race was the one that created mankind over 125,000 years ago, and we came here because we saw that this planet was full of life, one of the very few planets like this in the galaxy. We saw that evolution was evolving two types of species, herbivores and carnivores. From the beginning we started to groom this planet for our eventual colonization of it, by forcing evolution to only favor carnivores so that these plants do not have to die to fuel the endless circle of life. However, when we left evolution started ticking on its own again regardless of our intervention. Omnivores were evolved into this planet's gene pools, omnivores that contained some of our DNA but were far removed from us. We have returned to reclaim our new home, to cleanse this planet of those who wish to destroy its nature

Wen: could we not just live in harmony, the thing with our species is that we can change our diets at will, only be herbivores

Kiola: that is not the only thing that we were worried about, we were also worried about the desecration of the landscape, the beautiful skies, the clear blue oceans, etc. Your technology ruined it, you've defiled the landscape, and everything that makes this planet habitable for us

Xertaif: so, what is your request then

Kiola: my request is to peacefully dismantle all of your infrastructure, all of it

Xertaif: we can't do that, we're living beings just like you, please we can come to an understanding

Kiola: what understanding do you propose

Xertaif: why don't we just designate a part of the planet where your race can live

Kiola: that does sound quite tempting. However, I have studied up on human history. Humans have a natural tendency to be hostile either verbally or physically to a race that is not like them, like, what was it, segregation from the 1920s or whatever it's called

Xertaif:....you do realize that, that whole thing was almost 1000 years ago right now right

Kiola: what about the race war of 2020

Xertaif: dude, that was like 700 years ago. That's changed, especially with the cultural shift of 2700

Wen: which kind of unfolded the same way the cultural revolution in china did back in the 1950s

Kiola: you know what. Fine, I'll take you up on that offer, I call off my surfs, and relinquish control of their minds back to them

Maein: wait, you mind controlled those people to become terrorists?!

Kiola: yes, you got to understand, though my race may look shockingly human, we can control various types of plants, and use spores to mind control other living creatures

Maran: ooof, cliché

Kiola: Haven't you always wondered where all those clichés came from in the first place. Your DNA is encoded with memories that we passed down to you when we created your genus

Maiora:....

Xertaif: don't....say.....it

Maiora: aaaaaaa

Xertaif: say it and no coffee for you for the rest of the week

Maiora: aw ok

Maran:ASSASSIN.. **Wen slaps her upside the head**

Wen: anyways. How is that possible, the science says that memories can't be directly passed down through natural means

Kiola: that is because by the time you discovered what you call science, your gene pool has mutated enough and gone through the cycles of evolution for long enough to no longer carry that property

Xertaif: whew, crisis averted

Kiola: do note that under my hive-mind control over my army, some people have accepted the whole destroy all humans ideal as a way of life, so be prepared to still face insurgent resistance

Wen: to be honest, I thought this whole negotiation was going to be much harder to do

Kiola: I thought so too, with my studies of human history I thought we would need to settle this the way humanity has always settled things; by war

Xertaif: see, humanity has changed. Yes, we've had 3 world wars in our existence....and a fair bit of civil wars...but with each war, each struggle and each division, we learned, bit by bit that we can't just think about ourselves anymore - we have to think about everyone. As the famous Emora Sovinsky once said

Xertaif, Wen, Vas, Fidel, Maein, Maran: All living things deserve the best treatment.

Kiola:.........then I think we'll take you up on your offer to live in peace with this race, integrate back into the fold, so-to-speak. I'll send for my Entourage immediately, they'll be so glad that their queen has befriended another race

Wen: wait....queen?

Kiola: ah yes, my race operates in sort of a similar fashion to your human monarchies, and I just so happen to be its ruler

Xertaif: huh, whelp, welcome to earth

Kiola: you're not going to do smithing?

Xertaif:...wait what?

Maiora:.....oooooooooohhh I get it, movie cliché

Xertaif: ooooooohhhhhh, well I don't mean it in a hostile way, I genuinely, on behalf of the governments that are still left on this planet, I welcome you

A phone can be heard ringing

Xertaif: hold on a second……hello?

Vertis: we have an issue here!

Xertaif: what is it!?

Vertis: we just got a distress signal from the Zeus, it seems to be on its way back from Trappist1e, and it appears to be a low crew signal

Xertaif: low crew? Where could the crew possibly…….oh no……Kiola, do you have any information on this

Kiola: while I still had control over my army, I had 1 impostor aboard your primitive vessel under the name Eiensta Marrik, he was promptly ejected out of the air lock after the crew did some social deduction

Xertaif: Vertis, who is the alive crew member

Vertis: it's commander Cevko, and who is this Kiola?

Xertaif: I'll explain later…Kiola, do you know Cevko

Kiola: I do not know a commander Cevko, I've never had that name in my hive mind at all

Xertaif: so that means that there was something extremely hostile on Trappist1e, which can't be possible. We sent a probe there in 2100 and got it back in 2600……

Kiola: I suppose I should relay this information, the actual organization that was able to carry out attacks orchestrated by me has some dedicated followers that will either hire mercenaries or try to destroy humanity themselves

Xertaif: can't you just re-mind control them and make them not want to blow us up

Kiola: my hive mind spores only work one way - I can influence and/or out-right control another living creature with poor mental defense, but I can't reverse that because if I do, it's a 100% chance to kill them. I am truly sorry that I ended up doing this. I guess I fell victim to the human blunder of shoot first ask questions later

Xertaif: don't worry, we'll get through this, humanity has dealt with worse

CHAPTER V SUBVERSION

It has been one year since that last conversation we saw in the last chapter. That race that Kiola was part of has settled on earth and have already for the most part integrated into the wider population which made humanity more empathetic to the nature that surrounds them. However, that rogue state, that insurgent group that kept the mentality of humans to be bad were doing regular campaigns, none of them peaceful. In the meantime, let's check on the status on everything aboard the U.U.W. Zeus

Cevko: this is Asterbo Cevko. Quantum resonators active, sending entanglement request

Receiver: Penotargo Zenkaio mukauti

Cevko: viopyma meoa zarak

Receiver:Moailaentais. Report

Cevko:
Time: 12:00
ETA: 2 years
Status: Healthy and ok
etc.

Receiver: What is the status of the mission?

Cevko: Specimens secured in the cargo hold. They were hard to subdue, but modified shock collars have kept them in check thus far

Receiver: information about specimens

Cevko: there are 10 in total
gender split 50/50

average blood type O-

average height 1.4 meters

DNA type: random wound

DNA Sequence: Pseudo

Some scuttering can be heard

Receiver: Asterbo, what was that?

Cevko: that happens sometimes, it's due to sudden acceleration. Anyways, carrying on report

Meanwhile in the cargo hold

Triessians: **they're just lying on the ground and looking sad yet angry at their current situation**

Zara: **whispers** hey!

Triessians: **they get up and growl at her a bit, like they're about to start trying to attack her**

Zara: hey hey, calm down. I'm here to help you - well, keep you company. Just so you understand, he's the second imposter that was brought aboard this ship, you know all those classes you took, and all the assessments you took part of. That was just to survey how you work, but we tried to befriend you. Lieutenant Ryan, Carrie, Chase, and Roger wanted nothing more than that. However, they're dead and we're stuck here. All I want to do is to stay somewhere he won't look too often, so that I can stay alive

Triessian: **a lone Triessian walks up to her** are you sure you're not lying to us, we've been very trusting thus far, and now look at where we are

Zara: you must know intent, right, psychic and all

Triessian:...fair point, and you don't seem to have a bad intent. Can you please get us out of here?

Zara: not right now, if I were to try and tamper with anything those shock collars would not only send an alarm to the bridge, but also would cut off your heads, best I can do is at least comfort you for the two-year ride

Triessian2: two?…two god damn years

Zara: this ship is travelling at 50% or so the speed of light, aided with a slight quantum folding effect it's not quite warp speed like those old sci-fi movies use to talk about, but it's faster than just pure gravity assists and boosting like crazy.

Triessian2: at least we have company

Zara:….why aren't the rest of you talking

Triessian: the others are tired and scared. They fear that if they speak too loudly the collars might pick it up as a bark.

Zara: well, since both of you seem to be ok, how about I name you

Triessian: we already have names

Zara: oh? What are they?

Triessian: I'm ZoshienIkajiozian

Triessian2: and I'm Kaizolokaizo

Zara:……well I can't pronounce them, so how about I give you nicknames. Zoshien….whatever, how about I call you Noai

Noai: oooooo, that's a good name

Zara: and Kawldo, whatever, how about I call you Xendo

Xendo: A. that name sounds generic, and B. what's so hard to pronounce Kaizolokaizo, it's literally Kaizo but twice

Zara: it's just so that I can say your names quicker

Xendo: whatever

The ship shudders a bit and gravity momentarily shift directions

Zara: retro boost, damn we're past the 1-year mark. Anyways, get comfy, I will look around to see if there's any munitions around, just to make this next 2 years go by quickly.

Yet another time skip, this time to when the U.U.W. Zeus is within 1000km of earth, on a steady retrograde trajectory into high earth orbit

Receiver: Asterbo Cevko, we read you loud and clear, trajectory nominal, Delta V nominal, prepare of pre-emptive ejection

Cevko: aye, will acquire a male and female specimen for pre-emptive ejection

Cevko then heads to the cargo hold, opens the cage of Triessians, and uses his control pad to basically force a random male and random female Triessian to exit the cage. He then closes the cage back, and proceeds to force them to the escape pod bay

Triessian: GRRRRRRRR

Cevko: nuh uh uh, bad doggy **activates his shock collar**

Triessian:ARF, ARF,

Cevko: I didn't want to do this, but you leave me no choice **heads to turn his voltage up**

Zara: OH NO YOU DON'T **tackles him and his control pad hits the ground, which spooks those Triessians into the nearest escape pod**

Cevko: why you little…..huh?....heh **punches the escape pod eject button and presses the evacuate button**

Zara: wait WHAT!

Cevko: **punches Zara right in the face and tries to aim her in the direction of the open escape pod airlock**

Zara: AHH **returns that punch, and round house kicks him in the side of the head, and jabs him hard in the gut**

Cevko: **gets stunned with that last blow and is staggering back into the airlock**

Zara: DIE **kicks him out of the airlock and quickly closes it** damnit, where the hell did that escape pod go.

There's faint radio chatter in the bridge, so she picks up his control pad, and unlocks the cage and unlocks all the shock collars

Zara: hello, who is this

Receiver: OH SHIT, SHUT IT DOWN

Then silence

Zara: damnit. Let me see…….mission control, do you copy

………………

Zara: Mission control, this is lieutenant Zara Uiomwe of U.U.W Zeus, please respond

………………..

Zara: I am in high earth orbit and retrograde thrusters have been de-activated and I can't activate them, please respond

Mission control: this is mission control, we read you loud and clear Lieutenant Uiomwe. Taking remote control of the craft. Retrograde thrusters activated and are at full power, T minus 1 hour to stable low earth orbit. We will send a rescue team to collect you……scans indicate 8 other life forms, disclose

Zara: We met the natives of Trappist-1e-2, they're a kind of hyper intelligent K-9

Mission control: that is against space conduct article XIV

Zara: We had no choice, Commander Cevko was an imposter, and seemed like he wanted to collect these creatures for some reason.

Mission control: alright, talk it out with the president. Dispatching rescue team now.

Upon arriving back on earth, she expects to be arriving back at the White House in Washington DC, but instead, the rescue shuttle flies to Antarctica to the backup presidential bunker

Secretary of state: Mr.President, one of the operatives aboard the U.U.W. Zeus has arrived

Xertaif:well, what are you waiting for, get them in here

Zara: Mr.President?

Xertaif: ah, Lieutenant Uiomwe…what happened to the rest?

Zara: they were killed by the impostor that was reported to be on board, commander Cevko. The full report should be on your holopad

Xertaif:…and what are these two dogs you brought with you

Xendo: we aren't normal dogs you jackass

Xertaif: woah, hey sorry, yeesh…also talking dogs!?

Zara: they're natives to Trappist-1e-2, again, the report has that information

Xertaif: why not tell me now? Why in such a hurry?

Zara: because I want to know why this meeting isn't taking place in the White House

Xertaif: that I'm afraid is classified

Maiora: **walks in with 3 cups of coffee** it just means he wants to dodge the question. The reason why we're in presidential bunker SP-21a is because of coups

Zara: a coup? what the hell happened while I was gone?

Xertaif: **sigh** fine let me explain.

If you remember from before the expedition, there was a minor insurgent force that was trying to not only take down the various governments around the world, but also was trying to exterminate the human race in the process. For the longest time, we had no clue why they were trying to do so, that is, until their leader, Kiola Arrondol

Zara: wait she's the first lady!?

Xertaif: yes, but let me finish…where was I, oh right **ahem**

Their leader who calls herself Kiola to personify herself in English, contacted us and was ready to declare all out war, mainly because of what she studied about human history. The story there is that her race was the one that created us. They came here to earth in the ancient past to try and prevent herbivores from existing because of their utter infatuation with nature, mainly plants, scenery etc. Their escapades of genetic engineering eventually ended up letting the evolutionary tree to create us as an off shoot. They only came back now because in usual space travel fashion it takes a hell of a long time when there is no quantum physics BS helping. The Queen of that race was the one that came to earth and used her powers of mind control to raise an army to overthrow humanity and destroy all the buildings, infrastructure, etc. so that earth could revert back to the state it was back before we existed.

During that meeting, we came to an understanding - we exchanged ideas on a truce or agreement on their goals. The reason why they did all that stuff to earth in the first place is because they were grooming it for their eventual colonization, and of course we came along and took that dream from them. The understanding we came to was that a large portion of the planet, usually places that either not many people live or we haven't expanded to yet were reserved for them. In exchange we don't get exterminated. However, a rogue portion of her army still wanted to carry out that prime directive set out for them. That was 3 years ago. I bet you can guess how she became the first lady

Zara:....right........so basically, the government has fallen?

Xertaif: yes and no. Kiola was the one that managed to get us out because she was able to temporarily mind control the invaders, but for some reason she couldn't keep control of them, like they were being mind controlled by another entity. That's why she's currently in the on-base hospital

Zara:.....well damn, we leave for 6 years and things go to hell. Right, so, what's the plan

Xertaif: we don't have much in the way of militaries left, so we converted them into special ops agents

Zara:....we?

Xertaif: Wen, Vas, and I

Zara: what about my father?

Xertaif: he was killed. The sad reality is that the leaders of all major countries that could not defend themselves are all dead

Zara:........

Xertaif: I understand how hard it is hearing that while you were gone your father was killed. I recently found out that my mother was killed in a similar fashion. She was the only one that did not make it out of the invasion

Zara: DAMNIT!!!

Maiora: coffee?

Zara:....**sigh** sure

Maiora: also, if it comforts you, we're looking for their base right now. As said earlier, we have spies, satellites, sonars, radio telescopes, etc., looking for them.

They hear some shouting in the next room over

Noai: what's that?

Xertaif: oh, that's the situation room for the space division; we're planning to set up a secret base in Luna Terrestrium

Zara:.....so you're saying you don't already have one there

Xertaif: it was set up after world war III, after the void of arms treaty, we cannot set up any military installation on another planet unless it's for the greater good and it's an emergency. We already have construction freighters delivering supplies to the other planets as we speak. I think they're just having some issue figuring out how to make a habitable living space on Saturn, Jupiter, and Uranus, seeing as they are gas giants

Xendo: maybe we can help?

Xertaif: forgive me for being rude, but what does a couple of dogs know about interplanetary travel and sustainable life support systems and/or terraforming

Xendo: well, we can learn about that like we learned your language

Noai: and we also can provide the manpower so-to-speak, because of our abilities

Maiora: they are correct sir, based on the reports from Trappist-1e-2, and the physicals and examinations we've done on the rest of the Triessians indicates that they do have what we need in order to efficiently build bases on other planets. We've already employed some on the search for the insurgent base.

Xertaif: I highly doubt we're going to find it this way, based on how many ways we've been searching for them. They either don't exist, we're fighting an enemy within, or they're using such an unusual encryption system that we can't detect it

Noai: have you tried looking for analog signals?

Xertaif: yes. I've had this talk with my cousin already. We already ruled out that if they even are transmitting anything to their operatives, then even technologies from over 100 years ago should still be picked up.

Xendo: watch how they're just using pen and paper to get around your bullshit

Zara: ha ha, checkmate, that's exactly what they're doing. I thought it was unusual that I even saw paper on the ship, and now I realize it was an off the grid way for Lieutenant Marrik and Commander Cevko to communicate

Xertaif:..........damn.....galaxy brain strats. If that's the case, then we can't trace them, our spies are the last thing we have

Secretary of defense: sir, incoming news from Colonel Irun

Xertaif: what is it?

Secretary of defense: here, watch this

Holds out a holocorder and plays the message on it

Holocorder: playing last received massage

Irun:
Sierra Alpha Foxtrot Epsilon

Reporting,
Time: 00:01
Status: undercover

This is day 4 of being an operative for the insurgent group that calls itself Nature's Hand. The leader who calls himself The Groom of Nature has announced their latest idea. Yesterday they seem to have gotten some strange specimens that appear to be K-9 in nature. They plan on using their DNA as a basis for a bioweapon. Enclosed in this message is the current plans for its production, because I was one of the scientists assigned to work on this bioweapon. I've gotta go now, they're doing a roll call

He then goes off the recording area for the holocorder, and a gunshot is just heard

Xertaif: what the hell! Could you trace where this call was coming from!?

Secretary of defense: that's the thing, the signal appears to be distorted in a similar fashion to a reflection

Xertaif: find out where that reflection came from! Damnit that means that they might be off planet

Noai: no……….I can feel that signal still

Xertaif: wait, what

Secretary of defense: huh? **Taps on the holocorder and another recent message is displayed**

Irun: **when the hologram appears, he's heavily breathing and appears to be severely injured** this is colonel irun……..they've found me out……..before I go, the location is **a flash is seen to his right, to his left where the wall was nice and clean is now covered in blood and brains**

Noai: it's orbiting the earth

Xertaif: no…no….NOOOOOOOOOO

Zara: what?

Xertaif: it's the United Space station. Its comms can only reflect off the moon, because it was the most efficient way to get 1 transmission to everywhere on earth

Xendo: well, what are you waiting for, send dudes with guns to pew pew them down

Noai: Can you not be so reckless? if there's a bioweapon aboard, then going in recklessly might release it

Xendo: don't be so naïve. He said it wasn't done yet, so there's a chance, and plus I have way more experience at logic than you do

Noai:…..what's that supposed to mean

Xendo: just yes

Noai:……ok

Xertaif: that dog

Zara: her name is Noai

Noai: well, it's not, but my actual name is too hard for humans to say, so I'll stick with Noai

Xertaif:…ok, Noai has a point, we can't risk that bioweapon breaking out. Anyone know the status of Special agent Arven?

Secretary of defense: he's dead as well, but he appears to have died more recently than Irun. He was caught transmitting the genome of the weapon to us, and the fact that they're already doing tests of the bio weapon on the general populace.

Xertaif: a-already!?

The meeting room holo projector turns on

Wen: Xertaif, get control of your country!

Xertaif: I can't. I was booted out

Wen:...damn, well you can try talking to your citizens now. The so called King of the united states killed himself; I suspect it's this pathogen our scientists have discovered

Noai: woah, who's that

Wen:.....what the

Xertaif: I'll explain later, we have information on the pathogen, it's a bioweapon by that insurgent terrorist group based on these K-9's DNA. Maiora

Maiora: yes sir

Xertaif: patch me through to the US broadcast systems

Maiora: right away sir

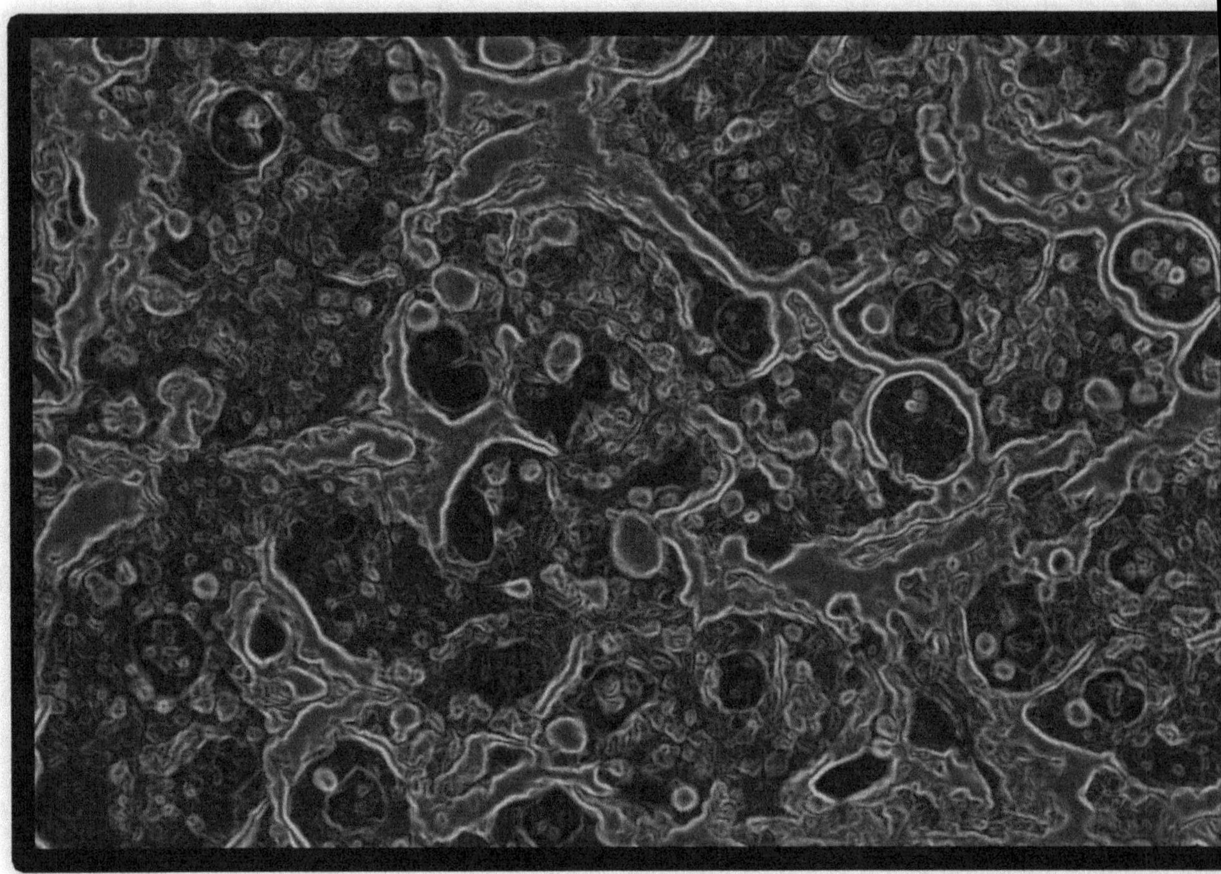

CHAPTER VI INFECTION

Xertaif: are we live?

Maiora: yes sir, all citizens can see and hear you now

Xertaif: alright **ahem**

My fellow Americans, I understand that this country is in shambles and in dis-array right now...especially following the recent incidents of our government being destroyed by these terrorists. As you can see, I am alive and well, and the government is here as well. I do not know when I'll be able to return, but I can still provide guidance and hope for all of you listening right now.

It is right now that I must deliver some very somber news. Recently we have gotten information from un-disclosed sources about what this terrorist organization is doing. They have released a bioweapon upon the populace. I urge you all to stay inside, and don't attempt to leave your houses. I'll be enacting an executive order to formally deactivate all human police and ban all people from being able to go into stores. We have online ordering, and drone deliveries for a reason, so use them.

I understand that an abrupt change in your routines like this is uncomfortable, and in a lot of cases people will not like it. If anyone is opposed to this new regulation, then feel free to go out and be infected. We have no clue what the pathogen can do, and please, for the love of all that is good do not make this a repeat of the 2020 global pandemic. Do not blame anyone as there is no one to blame, follow the rules as they are there to keep you safe and not to get rid of your freedoms. We'll be disclosing more information as we get it, as right now, we don't have much information on it besides that it's a bioweapon. This is president Arrondol signing off

Maiora: you do realize that the 2020 pandemic is what made people understand that lockdowns isn't a freedom thing right? Because people wouldn't listen to the qualified health professionals and thought that the virus present then wasn't real…those people ended up not living past that year

Xertaif: look, I know how my country acts, since 2100 it's tried to change, but it'll never change in a lot of ways, so I have to make these rules extremely strict

Maiora:….well shit, people are already protesting to allow them to leave their houses

Xertaif:……you know what, let them burn, I tried, but they clearly won't listen to reason

1 month passes and people in America are acting like they did in 2020, ignoring CDC guidelines, and thinking that this virus doesn't exist….however that can't be further from the truth. In literally 1 month this virus has killed 100 million people, and thus after that month people actually started to take this seriously seeing as there's no treatment for this at all, literally 100% of people infected with it has died in the most horrible ways ever

Xertaif: damnit! Damnit! Damnit!!!!

Kiola: calm down honey, it's not that bad

Xertaif: not that bad! This thing has killed 100 million people in one month, and none of our research teams even have a lead on this besides on how it transmits.

Dr.Zochi: Sir

Xertaif: Zochi

Dr.Zochi: we have a new extremely worrying lead on this virus

Xertaif: what is it?

Dr.Zochi: well, for starters the transmission is super diverse. It can transmit via water, air, droplets, contact, and passed down to fetuses.

Xertaif:..w…what's the other news

Dr.Zochi: oh, it can't be cured because it's not a traditional virus. See, a traditional virus just injects it's DNA into a healthy cell and replicates through that medium…..ordinarily as well that cell would destroy itself to protect the other cells in the body and the white blood cells would try to destroy that pathogen. However, this virus seems to have analogous DNA. It seems to integrate with the specific parts of human DNA that make it human, and cause it to break down over time, sort of like cancer but instead of making the cells replicate like crazy it makes them degenerate. One of the most active sites for this phenomenon is the brain

Xertaif:………so what about trying to boost the immune system

Dr.Zochi: well see, normally when the white blood cells attack a virus, they release cell receptors that get stored in various places around the body so they have memory on fighting the virus. This pathogen has its own answer to white blood cells, and can turn the white blood cells into zombies

Xertaif: so like HIV but even more devastating…..I'm guessing our HIV vaccine won't work then

Dr.Zochi: well it'll prolong the infected individual's life, but not by much. What's even more curious is that the virus can be carried by animals, but they don't exhibit any symptoms, their immune systems don't attack it, and it doesn't attack them, it's only active when in human cells

Xertaif:……..an un-curable virus….and it'll only mutate to be more deadly

Dr.Zochi: that's why I came to you Mr. President. My team has an idea on how to combat this

Xertaif:…oh?

Dr.Zochi: the only way to find a cure for this virus is to allow the virus to be in a human-like environment but without any of its effects coming to fruition

Xertaif: isn't the 700 million-dollar labs enough?

Dr.Zochi: no, the virus is able to tell if it's being examined in a lab and won't do anything. It can only be examined while it's in action, and specifically in action

Xertaif: can you not use the genome data we recovered from the space station?

Dr.Zochi: well yes and no. The genome of this virus is so complex that even if we were to make a vaccine now, it'd be instantly deemed useless with the rate of mutation this virus has, and again, it has its own anti-bodies that make the virus immune to a vaccine

Xertaif: so what's the full plan then

Dr.Zochi: we need to make a space station, a very heavily guarded one that no one but us can enter. It needs some of the best sanitation that can be offered, and some of the best labs in the world.

Xertaif: ok, we can certainly get on that

Dr.Zochi: it also needs to be able to basically fit the population of earth on it

Xertaif: why?

Dr.Zochi: projections indicate that all of humanity will have been destroyed by the time we find a cure, so we need to either bring people with us away from the virus, or, in worst case scenario it becomes the new home for mankind.

Xertaif: damn, that bad huh

Dr.Zochi:…yep

Xertaif: well, most of the world's governments are back in business now because those terrorists left when they released this damned thing. I'll get on a meeting with the world council and I'll see what they can do

Dr.Zochi: ok, I'll start rounding up a large team of the greatest minds this planet has to offer. I suggest that you and your cabinet get off planet now, with the likelihood of infection being non-zero, we need you alive

Xertaif: I'm not leaving until we can make sure people can stay safe

Dr.Zochi: ok then Mr. President, see you on the other side

Xertaif: see you too.

Dr.Zochi leaves the room

Kiola: should I contact the construction team to see if they can spare any manpower?

Xertaif: no, let the other countries handle this. Our plan is just a back up

Kiola: we got to let them know at some point

Xertaif: I already did, but I made sure not to provide many details on why I need their brightest scientists

CHAPTER VII SETTLEMENT

Let us catch up with what's actually been happening in all those time skips. Obviously Kiola became Xertaif's wife (mainly because they sort of bonded over Xertaif teaching her about proper human history), and there's also a settlement of not just Kiola's race, but the Triessians. This chapter is going to focus on the Triessians, and what they have to endure on earth because they're being blamed for the virus.

Noai: **just in her house, reading a book**

Xendo: **walks into her house and looks kind of pissed** damn humans

Noai: what happened now

Xendo: I was just trying to get groceries, but I was shooed out because they thought I was going to give them this stupid virus

Noai: are you sure it's blaming us, or is it because we look like the dogs on this planet, and the stigma of dogs here is that they tend to cause trouble

Xendo:oh, they know exactly what I am, they literally said "get out of here you mangey mutt, we don't want a 100% lethal virus"

Noai:...also are people just not listening to Xertaif? No humans at all should even be working

Xendo: it's robots controlled by humans, and they wanted me to leave because, they're robots, they have to be fixed, and they supposedly don't want it to be covered in germs

Noai: just calm down, have some cookies I made

Xendo: I DON'T GIVE A DAMN ABOUT YOUR COOKIES. DON'T YOU UNDERSTAND THAT WE'RE THE TARGET OF HUMAN RIDICULE? WHY THE HELL ARE WE BEING BLAMED AND NOT THE PLANT PEOPLE THAT LITERALLY MADE THE VIRUS

Noai: Seriously, calm down. You gotta understand, this is a natural human reaction, people start blaming other people

Xendo:SHUT UP. THIS WAS MEANT TO SUPPOSEDLY BE SOLVED ALMOST 100 YEARS AGO, AND NO ONE IS GOING TO LISTEN TO REASON

Noai: just wait a bit and eventually they'll understand

Xendo: grrr!!!

Noai: look, just take the damn cookies, I know chocolate chip is your favorite

Xendo: whatever. Oh, also why the hell is our race so boring

Noai: because it's a matter of perspective

Xendo: oh my god, STOP BEING SO CRYPTIC. REMIND ME WHY I LIVE WITH YOU AGAIN

Noai: because I'm your sister, and I can construct things better than you

Xendo:grrr, can I have extra chocolate in my cookies

Noai: sure

An explosion near their house is heard

Xendo: what was that?

Triessian: QUICK, GET HIM

Rogue Soldier: **just running away, and has some weird shield that blocks psychic waves, and presses a button on a detonator, and thus stuff starts blowing up a lot**

Xendo: Tyiokankei, what the hell happened

Tyio: how have you not noticed that this is the 3rd attack this month!?

Xendo: because we have outer defenses?

Tyio: whatever, it seems that the eco-terrorists that made this virus are trying to kill us off, because why the hell not

Xendo: are you sure it's not the other humans that just want to blame us for actually creating the virus, even though we had nothing to do with it, and they clearly know that it's those nutters?

Tyio: you say you have ties with the president of the united states?

Xendo: yeah, though he's kind of a dunce

Tyio: you think anyone that's not a Triessian is stupid

Xendo: am I wrong?

Tyio: sadly no. Anyways, take your sister and find where the president actually is

Noai: he's not in his house of leadership

Xendo: and how may I ask, do you know that?

Noai: we have a TV for a reason, and they seem to be doing some state of the union stuff with what looks like the president of China and the president of Russia

Xendo: ok, where is it then?

Noai: based on where the signals I feel seem to be coming from, it appears to be coming from somewhere in the middle of the ocean. I suspect that they have a man-made island there

Xendo: ok, how the hell do we get there

Tyio:........and you call other people stupid

Xendo:...wha?

Noai: we can fly, because this planet has less gravity than our home planet

Xendo:.....why did no one tell me this

Noai: because you would've continued to be pissed if we told you

Tyio: and you're literally on the service committee, did you not notice how there's some rules and regulations on flying

Xendo: I thought it was a joke

Noai:........**grabs xendo with psychic powers, and throws him into the nearest lake**

Xendo:AHHHHH!!!!!!!!

Noai: that should cool you off 😐

Xendo: GRRRRRRRRRR **makes a tidal wave in said lake**

Tyio: **disables his powers for a bit** you forget that I can do that

Xendo: screw you all, let's just go before I kill someone

Noai: why are you always so angry

Xendo: BECAUSE PEOPLE WONT STOP PISSING ME OFF

Noai: **shoves a chocolate chip cookie into his mouth**

Xendo:MMMMMMMMMMMMMMMMMMM...mmmmmmmm

Noai: works every time

Xendo: **he starts eating that cookie, and basically starts acting like an actual puppy**

Tyio: aren't we not meant to be eating chocolate?

Noai: we're not actually K-9, the human scientists have given us the genus Z-9, and thus not actually allergic to chocolate.

Tyio: whatever, take your brother and find someone that can stop this bull crap. If there's 3 world leaders in one place, they must know how to stop this

Noai: after he eats his cookies….he's weirdly obsessed with them.

CHAPTER VIII STATE OF THE UNION

Wen: Nihao, Konichiwa, Bonjour, Ciao, Zdravstvuyte ,Halo, Hello people of the world. Welcome to the 10th meeting of the United World Emirates.

Usually when this committee meets, it's usually in the name of life, liberty, and the pursuit of happiness, to move mankind forward and to make the world as a whole a better place. I find it saddening that we have met under these circumstances, as my ancestor Wen Maizhou helped form this global alliance for the sole purpose of protecting what is dear to us, and to keep us moving forward, and to make the hard decisions together.

This is why I solemnly have conducted this meeting to address the state of this union. As many of you have noticed, there was a rogue element whose purpose was to destroy humanity, and dismantle all mankind has done in the past 12,000 years, in the name of nature; the same nature that this committee was formed to protect in the first place. First, these terrorists dismantled our governments, though like those who came before, we bounced back. Now they have released a super virus onto the earth. A virus of the likes we've never seen, a virus that evolves, a virus that thinks, a virus that cannot be cured, and a virus that has only one goal, to kill humans. This is why this committee was called today, to better put into understanding the situation, and how we can combat this. I will hand of the stage now to those leaders who showed up, as you can clearly tell most can't even leave their houses, and places of leadership due to this crazy pandemic. Without further ado, I give the stage to my counterpart in the Kremlin, Vaschcroviz Ventriov

Vas: Hello people of the world. As Chairmen Wen has told you, this is the saddest most heart wrenching meeting that has been called in the history of this committee

I do not have much to add to what has already been said, but I will list the state of my country, as the leaders who could make it today intend to do, to put the whole situation in perspective, to allow each and everyone of you to be more informed, and to decide what is the best course of action to stay safe.

Thus far, in Russia alone, 10 million people are dead. This is even after a national lockdown with a stay-at-home order so strict that it might as well be imprisonment - people still died because they had no idea about a virus before it was already spread enough that the exponentials spiraled out of control. Those who are still alive, however, no longer have access to any essentials due to the sheer demand of sterile food, sterile water, as this virus can spread in so many ways that it all has to be sterilized four times over. This is why currently I have my top scientists working on trying to find some kind of cure for this damned virus. Now I give the stage to my comrade in the White House.

Xertaif: Thank you vas.

Hello my fellow world citizens, many of you may know me as just the 709th president of the united states, and most of you may know me as Xertaif Arrondol, but in this time of need, consider me as your friend and your neighbor. We need unity if we are to survive this like humanity always does.

The situation stands as this, in the United States of America 100 million people are dead, and with a country with a population of only 200 million people that's saying something. That means that between the numbers of dead in Russia, America, and China, almost a little under a third of the world's population is gone, just like that. There's even more bad news. Dr.Zochi, the head of the CDC, has disclosed to me that this virus has no cure - it's systems too complex for even our most powerful quantum computers to find a solution in time before mutation, its ability to actively fight a vaccine etc.

This is why I am formally asking the leaders of the world that couldn't make it to this committee meeting, whose work on rebuilding their governments has made attending holographically almost an impossibility but can still watch this live footage after the fact; I formally ask you to send your spare healthy people, your healthy scientists, healthcare workers, etc. to the U.U.W Ark. This is a space station which is under construction to bring an idea into fruition that the top scientists in all the countries around the world has come up with. We aim to give the greatest minds in our world's history a perfect environment to be able to research this virus, to see if we're missing anything. I understand that this information may seem bad, like we're abandoning humanity, and I've already received pushback on this idea by my own people. However I assure you that we have not given up on humanity – we simply are trying to provide the best chances on getting through this, and getting through it together. I hand the floor back to Wen

Wen: Thank you Mr. President

As you can see the situation is dire, even in my own country 1.5 billion people are dead. 1.5 billion lives that couldn't be saved, 1.5 billion lives that add on to the numbers already said by Vaschcroviz and Xertaif. A proportional amount of people have died in our countries, with Russia having 70% of it's population being dead. America with 50%, and China at 49%.

This is why this committee was formed, to bring us together and unite us against a blight like this. I'm unsure about the other leaders, but to all the people who are willing, Xertaif, Vaschcroviz and I have officially opened our space programs up to the public, those who are healthy, those who are willing, and those with knowledge can chose to step up to the plate; can chose to put your life on the line for the greater good, those of you who do will be remembered in history as the people that prevented the extinction of this brilliant species, those who fought the unbeatable, those who did the impossible. In the meantime, I will be personally seeing to it that military grade hazmat suits are distributed across the world. Unlike pandemics of days gone past, masks do not help, and we haven't had to innovate on this since 2020. This is why I believe this is the best option.

Remember this saying, "We all have limited time, it's what you chose to do in what time you have can make a difference and leave a legacy. Memento Mori"

Xertaif: wait, hold that thought

Wen: oh? What is it?

Xertaif: I just got some more information about this by Dr.Zochi. It appears that the virus appears to be force mutating non-human terrestrial species

Wen:....terrestrial? what!?

Xertaif: oh, I forgot to tell everyone this, and I think the state of the union is the best place to say this. A few months ago, the expedition to Trappist1e returned, and only one of its crew was alive and well. Another trick of those terrorists was to plant an impostor aboard the vessel. Along with it came a new species that call themselves Triessians.

Noai: woof

Wen: what the hell is a dog doing here, security

Noai: wait no! I was just trying to be funny on international television

Vas:......what in the hell

Xendo: I freaking told you not to interrupt this. It seems to be some important conference thing that the humans have to give each other some kind of comfort

Xertaif: **sigh** yeah, these are two members of the 10 specimens brought from Trappist 1e-2, they're hyper intelligent K-9 like creatures that appear to be immune to this virus, and based on the recent raid on the original U.U.W space station their DNA was also used as a basis for what we've dubbed Cerebral Necrosis

Noai: oh, hello all the humans in the world. This virus that they are talking about is super-duper nasty, like it melts your brain and crap, it's not good. Don't be a retard, stay inside and stay safe

Xendo: can you please not

Noai: what, I'm just saying

Xertaif: **sigh** ok Wen, we can sign off now before things get cringy.

Wen: sure, why not, anyways, that'll be all, this is Wen Jayzhou

Vas: Vaschcroviz Ventriov

Xertaif: Xertaif Arrondol

Wen, Vas, Xertaif: signing off.

Xendo: we're sorry for interrupting your important speech thing, she's just a bit over energetic because she's young

Xertaif: well, she does act like a puppy

Noai: I'm 90 years old

Xendo: and I'm 300, so quiet now

Xertaif: wait what

Noai: oh yeah, we live for a long time, the average life span for us is like 4000 years

Wen: so exactly what are you

Noai: we're called Triessians. We're the ones that came up with the name so before you say it violates any kind of grammar, it doesn't because English makes no sense

Xendo: Noai, let's head back home.

Xertaif: you can stay if you want - you can meet the other leaders of the world.

Noai: oooo, world travel **literally bounding around and wagging her tail like an actual puppy, but you know she's 90 years old**

Xendo: please ignore her, she's taken a liking to acting like those K-9 creatures you talk about

Xertaif: well the colloquial term is dog. K-9 is just the actual genus.

Xendo: so about this idea you have

Xertaif: the whole space station thing

Xendo: no, the other one

Wen: what other idea

Xertaif: nothing!

Vas: comrade, you don't need to hide anything from us

Xertaif: I'm not hiding anything!

Xendo: that's a lie

Xertaif: no it isn't!

Xendo: we can literally read your mind! Of course you're hiding something, just spit it out

Just before xertaif can start explaining himself because of the psychic doggo's psychic outing, there's a loud crash at the doors of the meeting room of the United World HQ. Suddenly, there's a bunch of soldiers whose uniforms look like the US military uniforms but not camouflage colored, instead they're random colors like someone just didn't care about the color scheme, but it's muted colors so it doesn't stand out like a sore thumb.
Before anyone can react, each leader present there and their various advisors etc, are being held at gunpoint.

Cevko: **walks in like he owns the place** well, I didn't expect for anyone to be outside of their little hidey holes. Heh, hey there yellow beauty, ya miss me

Wen: I'm going to kill you

Cevko: oh really, you and what army? I'm not the one being held at the end of an AR-15

Xertaif: c-cevko

Cevko: that is Absterbo Cevko to you "Mr.President"

Xertaif: I don't get it, why you

Cevko: because money speaks

Xertaif: what do you...

Vas: he's a traitor

Wen: wait, you know him!?

Xertaif: and you two know him!?

Cevko: we all have some history together. Obviously, you had no idea who I was because I was just the commander of that god forsaken ship, and beforehand I was a captain in your military...these two on the other hand

Vas: He was the one that tried to kill me a few years ago

Cevko: that was because I was being paid to do so, apparently you have a bunch of enemies

Vas: grr

Cevko: and you, aren't you going to explain our history

Wen:....

Cevko: heh, well it's your choice. I was her previous secret service equivalent, but I decided to try and escalate things, and usurp the title of chairmen from her. After all, being chairmen of a prosperous country would be a huge boon for me. Plus, I could've started a dynasty with her

Xertaif: what the heck is wrong with you? That's sick, and perverted!

Cevko: so, what. That was what humanity was like in the beginning

Xertaif: what do you mean?

Cevko: at the risk of sounding like a cliché, I wanted things to go back to the way it was before the 3rd world war. I was a young boy back then, but my father always wanted to go back to the military. He just didn't feel like he had a purpose other than to be a family man.
Yes, he was wealthy, and had 3 kids and a loving wife, but he wanted more. That's why world war 3 started, he wanted to feel the exhilaration of action again. He used his contacts to make the correct circumstances happen to cause world war 3.

Xertaif: w-what the hell

Cevko: Amazing, right? My father wanted a world of endless war because he was bored, and now I'm bored, and now I can start another world war. Boys, Kill those two, leave me the president of the united states

Wen: WAIT NO!

Soldiers: **pulls their triggers, but no bullets come out. Then they get suddenly thrown back against the wall. Some are just knocked out, and some are bleeding out because the various knives and ammo either stabbed them or went off in their utility belts**

Cevko: what the actual hell

Xendo: Surprise Motha fuka

Cevko: OH SHIIIIIT PULL BACK, PULL BACK

Naoi: they can't, We're holding them here. Now who's the one being held at gunpoint?

Cevko: **suddenly, he starts to choke up blood, and when he looks down, he sees a sword lodged in his chest with it's blade sticking out** w-w

Zara: this is for the crew of the U.U.W Zeus **presses a button on the sword and it makes a loud zapping noise, turning cevko into a pile of ashes.** You owe me one

Xertaif: Well, at least we're safe....I highly doubt that Cevko was the leader of the terrorists, but I do have a feeling he was the one that made this damn virus and basically changed a bunch of governments for the worst

Kiola: **goes to xertaif and hugs him** i-I'm sorry for making this in the first place

Xertaif: it's ok sweetie. It was 1 year ago, and you had no clue that some people were going to make their programming persist after you dropped your mind control

Wen: I am so glad he's dead, but now we have to continue the hunt for the real leader here. Plus we have to keep everything up and running in order for the skeleton to be built

Vas: we should head back to our countries, most likely news of this will get out, and we need to be in our houses of leadership in order to unify not only our nations, but this world. Stay safe comrades

EPILOGUE: THE LONG ROAD TO SALVATION

      Many months would pass as each country contributed to this massive scale project to help bring the perfect research facility ever made. It's a project that will take 100 or so years to complete, and many more years to bear fruit. While this is all happening, people continue to die and suffer. A virus designed to slowly reverse-engineer the cell, and make it useless to the organism; A virus that cannot be cured; A Virus that cannot be contained; A Virus that has already begun its plan of evolution.

      In the oval office a ringing phone is heard, this is the old red phone that was put in place around the time of the cold war, and hasn't been used since. However, it can still interface with modern tech because of conversion systems etc.

Xertaif: **picks up the phone** hello?...Speaking.....WHAT!? THAT'S IMPOSSIBLE

What's impossible you might ask, well. Find out next time.
Ugh, what happened
Oh no, he's back
Did you just write a book without any detailed paragraphs of what's currently happening in the scene?
You can look back through you know
Oh lord you did. What is wrong with you? There are no details on where these people are, why they're there, nothing. How can you call this a book if you do not have an overarching setting, or any kind of coherency between each chapter? Do not get me started on the time skips
You just overlooked basically half the book. Each chapter has a preamble paragraph, and each time skips happens because of the defined rules of this universe. Like how I said that it would take that damn ship 3 years to get to and from that pseudo fictional solar system, so I made it take 3 years, but obviously 3 years of literally nothing wouldn't be too interesting now would it
There was stuff going on in those 3 years, you could have wrote about that. Oh, and I hope you're happy with yourself; this book is only 48 pages long, and you don't seem to care about its length
Look, this stupid text formatting you chose isn't bloody helping with the page count - maybe next time chose something else
But this text size is the average text size for a book. It's what people expect from a book that's supposed to have a bunch of detail in it, and a lot of nuanced dialog. You failed in that regard, and thus this issue you're having with the text formatting is your punishment
Whatever, anyways. Reader, this is the end of this book. I know it's a cliff hanger, and I know it's a prequel book, but please, provide some feedback and read the other books in the series.

www.ingramcontent.com/pod-product-compliance
Lightning Source LLC
Chambersburg PA
CBHW081239130726
47997CB00009B/2937